"Thou hast done wonderful things."
—ISAIAH 25:1b

Thank You, God,

for Wonderful Things

By Ruth Shannon Odor
Illustrated by Frances Hook

Distributed by Standard Publishing, Cincinnati, Ohio 45231

THE CHILD'S WORLD
ELGIN, ILLINOIS 60120

Distributed by Standard Publishing, 8121 Hamilton Avenue,
Cincinnati, Ohio 45231.

Library of Congress Cataloging in Publication Data

Odor, Ruth Shannon.
  Thank you, God, for wonderful things.

  Slightly expanded ed. of the author's work published
(c1977) under title: My wonder book.
  SUMMARY: Thanks God for the pebbles, puddles, flo-
wers, and other small things in nature He has provided
for us to enjoy.
  [1. Nature—Fiction. 2. Stories in rhyme]
I. Hook, Frances. II. Title.
PZ8.3.O29Th   1980   [E]   80-16106
ISBN 0-89565-170-X

Thank You, God, for Wonderful Things

Oh, pretty, pretty butterfly,

I cannot catch you if I try.

But, oh, the colors of your wings —

They are such lovely, wondrous things!

Inchworm, inchworm,

Funny, little, green worm,

You arch your back as high as it goes,

Then stretch your head in front of your toes.

I wonder if you're traveling,

Or measuring,

Or just doing your exercises.

Hey! Look!

In the puddle!

All the pretty colors!

The oil on the water

Has almost made a rainbow!

Isn't it strange that a spider's web

Is such a lovely thing?

The strands go up and down and in and out;

They almost look like string.

The spider works so hard to make

His home with such design;

I wonder if, as he works, he has

The pattern in his mind.

The willow tree is my favorite,

The first to green in the spring.

To peep through its drooping branches

Is such a special thing.

Tiny, purple violet,

Hidden in the grass,

Do you know I almost

Stepped on you as I passed?

Your stem is, oh, so tiny;

Your petals, such a lovely color.

I think I'll take you home

And give you to my mother.

I love to lie in the grass,

So it is taller than I,

And watch it bending over

As the wind goes by.

Sand, sand, sand —

Tiny, little grains of sand.

I love to feel you with my hands

And walk on you in my bare feet

And wet you down

    And dig a hole

        And build 'most anything.

I found some strawberries in a box.

They smell so good to me.

I wonder how they taste —

Well, let's just see!

Brrr! The icicle is cold to hold

And clear as crystal glass.

Heat will make it disappear.

I know it will not last.

The song of a mockingbird

Is a wondrous thing to hear.

I wonder if he learns new songs

Every single year.

I am so glad I found you, little pebble.

I like to look at your color

And your roundness

And feel your smoothness

And toss you in the air

And take you home

To put in my box of wonderful things.

Such a lovely little feather,
With colors of black and blue.
I wonder why I found it
Underneath my shoe.

Did some little bird drop it
As he flew up high?
I wonder if he'll miss it
As he flies up in the sky.

They look like tiny drops of rain.

My daddy says they're dew.

Sometimes I see a lot of them;

And sometimes, just a few.

Dewdrop . . . dewdrop . . . dewdrop . . .

The name is like a song.

I'll watch the dewdrops on a leaf;

They won't stay very long.

Only God could make a butterfly

With beautifully colored wings,

Or a little, gray mockingbird

With so many songs to sing.

Only God could think up inchworms, dewdrops,

And tall green willow trees.

Purple violets, pebbles,

And sands beside the seas.

Thank You, God, for the wonderful world

That You have given me.

Thank You for all the wonderful things

To touch, and taste, and see.